BONNA NATALI

Bonna Natali was a negro surfer girl I met at Huntington Beach in 1963. We were both 14 years old.

I had been pacing with my surfboard along the water's edge, watching surfers.

I saw her stand up on a heaving breaker. Her hair was rippling down her backside.

She rode the surf up onto the inclined beach. She hopped from her board and picked it up and then she was splashing toward me.

She quickly nodded to me as she was passing.

Her skin was glistening.

I was aroused. She was a negro but she was the most beautiful girl I ever saw.

My mouth said, "Hi."

Then I was saying, "I haven't seen you around here before."

She stopped and turned around, saying, "I'm kind of hard to miss around all these bushy blonde hairdos, aren't I?"

I answered, "No. Yes…I mean, you're pretty good. …At surfing. …Hey, I'm Dean."

She said, "Hey, I'm Bonna… but they call me 'Zulu'."

I said, "Bonna is a pretty name. I like it."

She objected, "Call me Zulu. Only my family calls me Bonna."

I nodded, "Oh, sure, sorry."

She said, "That's Ok. Honkies used to call me 'Zulu' the way they called me 'Nigger'."

I winced.

She asked me, "Why are you embarrassed?"

I mumbled, *"That word.* My mom told me…"

She smiled wickedly, "You are a real virgin, aren't you."

I fumbled, "I was just surprised…," changing the subject to, "I'm from Long Beach. Where are you from?"

She replied, "Compton."

I continued, "My dad brings me here for me to surf while he studies for his business degree. That's him over there."

She said, "Mmm hmm."

I added, "I want to be a Marine Biologist. And I like The Beach Boys so I wanted to learn surfing."

She said, "Mmm hmm."

I added, "My buddy and me have a band. We're called The Surrrf Dawgs. You know, Rrrf, dogs, get it?"

Then to her silence I offered, "Hey, you want to get some corn strips and hot sauce? My treat."

She drew her head back and studied me and finally replied, "Why not?"

I said, "We can leave our boards with my dad," then I confessed, "I'll need to borrow some money from him, anyway."

We walked up to my dad who was sitting in his folding chair reading his big textbook, *Management Principles and Practices*.

We cast our shadows upon him and when he looked up I was saying, "Zulu, this is my dad."

"Dad," I said, "This is … Zulu."

My dad looked surprised, but he said, "Hello, …Zulu? How are you? Are you from South Africa?"

"Dad!" I felt myself blushing.

"Sport, that's where Zulus live." My dad smiled and gave me an odd look.

Zulu replied, unfazed, "My mother is from South Africa."

I intervened, "Dad, can I borrow some money for some corn strips?"

After a moment he replied, "OK. Here you go. Bring me back a *Bubble Up*, Sport. Nice to meet you, …Zulu."

She said, "Nice to meet you, sir."

We stuck our boards in the sand and we split for the snack stand.

I apologized, "My dad just says things like that."

Bonna said, "Mmmm hmmm."

I asked her, "How do you get here to Huntington Beach from Compton?"

She only replied, "I get around."

On the way to the snack stand I was noticing all the eyes directed at Bonna.

Bonna leaned against the snack stand counter nonchalantly. The three young guys manning the snack stand looked at each other and muttered, "Oogah Boogah!", and then they eagerly asked her what she wanted.

I answered them with what *we* wanted.

We got our two paper trays of corn strips and hot sauce, our two cups of iced *Coca-Colas*, and my dad's cup of iced *Bubble Up*.

As we walked back down along the shoreline I asked, "How long have you been surfing?"

Bonna replied, "Ever since my brother told me surfing was only for White People."

I was surprised and I said, "Surfing came from Polynesians."

Bonna retorted, "Colored People."

I was naïve. I explained, "Duke Kahanamoku was Hawaiian, but his buddy George Freeth Jr was the first white guy surfer, and they, like, introduced surfing right here at Huntington Beach back in 1907."

Bonna looked at me with one raised eyebrow.

Then I told her, "I go to Leland Stanford Junior High School. Have you heard of it?" and I felt like such a dweeb trying to make such geeky conversation.

Yet Bonna replied, "No. I go to Ralph Bunche Middle School. Ralph Bunche was the first negro to win the Nobel Prize."

I said, "Cool."

I finally ventured to ask, "Bonna, …Zulu, do you want to trade phone numbers so we can talk more later… sometime?"

Bonna considered.

Then Bonna knelt to the damp sand and set her corn strips and *Coca Cola* down. She wrote a phone number in the sand with her finger.

She rose up and said, "Your turn."

Taken by surprise, I etched my phone number below hers.

I was focusing hard to memorize her phone number.

Then the foam of a broken wave swiped away our correspondence.

We returned to my dad who was studying us as we approached.

I handed my dad's *Bubble Up* to him. He asked me, "Any change, Sport?" I handed him his remaining coins.

Bonna and I sat down on the sand and finished our snacks.

Bonna abruptly arose, brushed the white sand from her dark legs, and said, "Thanks. I got to go."

I stood up with her to say goodbye but she was waving to a negro guy in a jacket who was waving back to her from several yards up the beach.

Bonna plucked up her surfboard and she was gone.

My dad joked at me, saying, "You're always collecting sea creatures."

I said, "Her name isn't really Zulu. It's Bonna but she says that people called her Zulu."

Two days later I called the phone number that Bonna had written in the sand.

A woman answered.

I asked, "Hello, is Zulu there, please? This is Dean."

The woman on the phone clicked her tongue and said, "Lord. Whoever that damn girl is, she is laughing at all you silly boys."

She hung up curtly.

I was humiliated.

Two days later my mom answered a phone call and after a moment she said, "Yes, he is. Just a moment. Zulu?"

"Dean?!" She summoned me but I was on my way.

When she handed me the phone she teased me, "A girl? For you?"

My dad laughed.

I was excited and confused.

"Hi! I tried to call you!"

My dad warned, "Watch out, Sport. It's a woman."

I threw a "shush" at him as my mom slapped his shoulder.

Bonna was saying, "Meet at Huntington this Saturday?"

"Sure," I nodded.

When I hung up the phone I proclaimed, "Dad, I need a ride to Huntington this Saturday."

My dad said to my mom, "Our Sport is going to need some advice."

My mom said, "First of all, what kind of name is 'Zulu'?"

On that Saturday, Bonna found me out in the swells watching for a set of decent waves.

She called from behind me, "Hey, *Jiminy Dean.*"

I turned around to see Bonna sitting on her board. She was turned sideways pointing at some dolphins undulating past us several yards away.

I spoke excitedly, "Oh, wow, have you read *Man and Dolphin*?"

Bonna shrugged, "Why?"

I said, "This guy Lilly recorded two dolphins and he says they were talking in a language. A language of whistles and clicks and quacks and squawks!"

Bonna joked, "Two guy dolphins."

I smiled, "And Lilly says he's recording a library of their sound patterns so we can talk with them."

Bonna said, in a comically squeaky voice, "Like, *What's for dinner? Fish again?*"

I joined in, squeaking, "*Yes! Whitefish and Sole.*"

Bonna laughed like bells.

Suddenly Bonna turned her board around. She laid herself prone and began paddling to catch the momentum of the incoming set.

I dropped on my stomach and I paddled behind Bonna. Her butt was like a pair of black cherries.

Bonna brought her hands up from paddling and placed them below her chest, palms on the flat of the surfboard while her fingers curled over the sides.

In one quick motion, Bonna pushed her body up with her arms and tucked her feet up and under herself.

Bonna was graceful, like a wave herself.

Bonna put one foot where her hands pushed up from and put her other foot at a shoulder's width behind.

Then Bonna angled across the wave, turning her body, her long hair whipping.

I was only good enough to ride the wave straight in.

When the sets finally blew out, Bonna hollered, "That was rad! I'm going in."

I paddled back to shore behind her.

When I hit the beach Bonna was talking to that negro guy that I saw before. He was an older guy. He was wearing a jacket with a white shirt, black shoes, and no tie.

Bonna turned toward me and pointed. The negro guy glared at me and shook his head.

Bonna gestured for me to approach.

"This is my brother August," Bonna told me.

I was relieved but I was nervous. I smiled and I said, "Hi, nice to meet you."

August abruptly asked me, "Do you have any idea what's happening in Birmingham?"

I shook my head, "Birmingham?"

Birmingham was just a name to me. My dad had told me stories about being stationed in Birmingham during World War Two.

Donna was pleading softly, "August,…don't…"

August clenched his fist above his head and said, "Police dogs are attacking people who just want to be treated the same as you white Americans!"

Bonna protested, saying, "August, Dean is my friend."

August snarled, "He's trouble. And Dr. King is a chump for believing in non-violence."

Then August turned and walked away, saying to Bonna, "Come on. Let's get out of here."

Bonna frowned and shrugged to me as she left, following behind her brother.

I was confused but I was sure pleased to be "my friend".

When my dad saw me walking back toward him, he said, "Sport, you look bewildered."

I asked, "Dad, where is Birmingham, again?"

My dad hesitated and then he said, "Oh, boy, I was afraid of this."

On the drive home my dad began his old story, "Birmingham is in Alabama. I must have told you that I was stationed at the Birmingham Army Airfield in World War Two..."

Arriving home, my parents told me to watch the television evening news with them. They said, "Ask us any questions you have."

On the television, negro children and negro teenagers were marching through the streets of Birmingham, Alabama.

Then I saw negroes sitting on the sidewalk with hands behind their heads. Fire hoses were being turned on their backs.

The television guy said, "A Negro woman was bitten on the leg by a police dog. A Negro man had four or five deep gashes on his leg where he had been bitten by a dog. A sobbing Negro woman said she had been kicked in the stomach by a policeman."

I was alarmed. I asked, "Why are they doing this?"

My mom assured me, "This is all happening a long, long ways away from us here."

My dad explained to me in the same way he had explained to me about sex, "There are places where negroes have to… Where negroes have their own places… and white people have their own places."

I asked, "Why are they fighting?"

My mom answered, "Negroes just don't like staying in their places only. And other people don't like them not staying in their places only."

I said, "Bonna doesn't stay in her place. And her brother doesn't either."

My dad said, "Sport, if you and Bonna want to be friends you need to understand… That is … not really normal."

I stuck out my chin, saying, "What? I don't care."

My mom put her hand on my shoulder and said, "But there are people all around you who will care. Then you will have to care too."

My dad concluded, "You just have to become aware…to understand."

I was becoming aware, "You don't like her."

Quickly, both my mom and dad were talking, saying, "That's not really true." " We love you and we just don't want you to get hurt."

I said sarcastically, "Is a police dog going to bite me?"

My mom snapped, "You will see that it can be even worse."

I threatened, "I'm going to call Bonna."

My mom reminded me, "She didn't want you to have her phone number."

The next day I was in my room with my buddy John, rehearsing **The Surrrf Dawgs**.

John's family was Baptist like mine so I could tease him, calling him John the Baptist. He would then call me, "Deanie the Teeny Weinie."

That day I was distracted while we rehearsed. I was making mistakes during our song *The Devil Don't Surf*.

John stopped playing and said, "Bro', what is wrong? You're eatin' it here, fer sure."

I sighed dismally, "Yeah. Sorry. I'm tragic here. I met a honey surfing, and I really like her."

John perked, "Whoa, dude. Is she, like, a babe?"

I continued, "Oh yeah, but I really, like, *like* her."

John made a lewd gesture.

I said, "I mean it, you dork. I am 'way above that stuff. I'm on a crush and I'm falling down to love."

John looked at me skeptically, asking, "You think she could be The One?"

I sighed and I nodded affirmatively, "But it is so Romeo and Juliet, dude."

John asked, "Because you're Baptist and she isn't?"

I replied, "Worse."

John exhaled, "Whoa, bro'. What?"

I looked John in the eye,

John said again, impatiently, "What?"

I said carefully, "She is a hot *negro* beach bunny surfer."

John stared.

And then John burst laughing, "Only to you! Bro', you can't ever be normal."

And then John howled, "I bet you'll wear a black glove when you beat off!"

I was indignant but I had to laugh.

Bonna and I met again at Huntington a few days later. I told her that I had written a song for her called *Over the Falls*. She didn't seem to hear me.

Bonna said, "August is so angry. He's talking about a **revolution by black people. 'Let everybody** bleed a little bit,' he's saying. I am so bummed. He's arguing with my parents."

I said, "I'm sorry," meaning I was sorry to see Bonna bummed.

Bonna confided, "My whole family is Baptist but August says that he is going to join the Black Muslims. He's talking about 'black nationalism' and 'black separatism'. My father is worried that August will ruin his chances to get into medical school."

I offered, "We can talk whenever you want to talk."

Bonna sighed.

I said, "If I had your phone number…"

Bonna was emphatic, "Oh no. No good."

I asked softly, "Why?"

Bonna looked at me and said, "August doesn't like you. I don't want to make him more angry."

I looked around and asked, "Where is August anyway?"

Bonna looked toward the town, saying, "He's just walking around Huntington."

I said, "Come on, let's ride."

Bonna nodded but then she asked me, "What is *Over the Falls* about?"

I finally said, "Its about the way I feel. About you."

Donna turned and she pranced away into the surf, saying, "God help me," and she laughed.

I was glad to hear her laugh.

I dashed after her.

I thought that the beach was then just like us: She was the sea, I was the seashore. (When I told that to John he retched).

When Bonna and I were spent and we were paddling in toward the shore we both saw August being held between two policemen.

Once ashore, Bonna ran up to them, crying out, "What's wrong? August?"

One of the policemen said, "So you do know this gentleman?"

Bonna replied, "He's my brother. What's wrong?"

The other policeman said, "He's been accosting people."

Bonna asked, "Costing what?"

The first policeman clarified, "Approaching and addressing people aggressively."

Bonna asked suspiciously, "Addressing what?"

My dad was now approaching us at a concerned jog.

The second policeman advised August and Bonna, "Best if *you two* leave now."

August said angrily, "There is no moral distance between the facts of life in Huntington Beach and the facts of life in Birmingham!"

My dad arrived. My dad smiled at the two policemen and he put his arm around my shoulder and pulled me away, saying, "Come on, Sport."

I cried out, suddenly, "Bonna!"

Bonna said, "I'm ok. We're going home now."

August looked toward me and yelled, "Stay away from my sister, white boy!"

On the drive home my dad was saying, "I'm sorry, Sport. This is what your mother and I were trying to prepare you for. Just be glad this wasn't worse."

I asked, forlorn, "How long before I am going to see Bonna again?"

My dad said gently but quickly, "I think it's over, Sport."

I growled, "Nothing is over."

My dad looked at me with misgivings.

The next afternoon I was with John and I was entreating, "What can I do?"

John was smacking on a toast and honey sandwich. He smiled suggestively, saying, " I can always eat a *honey* sandwich."

John then smacked, "Dude, if she really is really, like, The One then sure there will be a way, I think. I guess…. Maybe."

I rolled my eyes, "Thanks, man, *I think, I guess, maybe.*"

John, his mouth full of toast and honey, spluttered, "Dude, your situation is…almost, like, biblical. And I don't, like, believe that even yours truly knows what to say. Sorry." John then concluded by slowly shaking his head, "It's a bummer. Talk about, like, uncharted coastline, dude…"

I bemoaned, "Its all up to Bonna. She has to call me. She's 15 miles away somewhere. Then I could take a bus…"

John said, "So could she, dude."

I realized, "Or I could use your motorbike…!"

John quickly put the kibosh on my thought, scoffing, "*Like hell* you'll take my cherry 'bike, dude!"

Then I hatched a desperate Plan Number Two, and I confided in John, "I could mope around the house until my parents bought me a motorbike to cheer me up. And then, if Bonna … when Bonna calls me…"

John said, "You are like, totally evil, dude. Good one. And if she tragically never ever calls, we can, like, cruise together. Hey, and you can teach *me* to surf."

I scowled, "Yeah, dude. That will be *totally the same*."

John held both palms over his heart, and performed in falsetto, "Oh, you, like, wound me, Romeo."

I critiqued his performance, "Fuck you, *Juliet*, you queer."

That night I dreamt I was hugging Bonna and it became a wet dream.

Weeks later my dad and I returned to our spot on Huntington Beach.

There, I experienced a miracle.

I unexpectedly saw Bonna standing with her surfboard at the shoreline. She was facing us. The ocean behind her sparkled in a sunshine halo.

I started to run to her with my surfboard. I heard my dad in exasperation say, "Shit."

I waved and I cried out, "Bonna!"

In a few moments I stood breathlessly before her and I said, "You came back. How are you? How did you get here?"

Bonna looked back up the beach and said, "My mother," and she waved.

Under a small beach umbrella sat an elegant negro woman. She waved back. She was wearing a long red, white, and black dress.

I turned back to Bonna and I said, "I am glad to see you. I am really glad your mother brought you."

Bonna said, "It was not easy. My father is worried for her. Because…of the way it is…"

I asked, "How did you convince them?"

Bonna replied casually, "I reminded them that I knew several boys with cars."

I asked uncertainly, "So why didn't you come with one of them?"

Bonna smiled wickedly and replied, "Next time I will."

Alarmed, I countered, "Your mom should meet my dad."

And thus I finally caught Bonna off guard.

Bonna laughed, "Oh, right."

I joined her laugh, suggesting, "We could tell them we're engaged."

Suddenly even the seagulls were silent.

Bonna warned, "My brother will be your Best Man."

I swore, "It's a joke!"

Then my dad was approaching and Bonna's mother was approaching.

In front of them neither Bonna nor I spoke at first.

My dad said to Bonna's mother, "Hello. I'm Dean's father. I'm Donald. Donald Johnston."

Bonna's mother nodded and said, "Nice to meet you, Donald. I'm Mrs. Natali, …Nandi, Bonna's mother."

My dad nodded and said, "Nandi, its… cute that these two share surfing."

Nandi agreed, "These two don't have a care."

My dad said, "Zulu is a very polite young lady."

Nandi said, "Her Christian name is Bonna. Zulu is her idea."

Bonna piped up impertently, saying, "Well, you are named Nandi after the mother of Shaka, King of the Zulus."

Nandi shook her head at Bonna and said to my dad, "She is prideful and headstrong."

My dad said, "Sometimes that is good," and then he looked at me and repeated, "Sometimes."

Nandi asked, "What can be done?"

My dad sighed and said, "Exactly. What can we do?"

Nandi recited, "*Their eyes already cross the full river.* That is a Zulu proverb meaning…," and then Nandi laughed, "*What can you do?*"

My dad finally asked Nandi, "Can we talk?"

Nandi agreed, "It is a good time."

My dad glanced at Bonna and me and asked Nandi quietly, "Alone?"

Nandi shook her head and replied, "These two probably need to hear what you will say."

My dad sighed and asked, "What do you think is happening? To this country?"

Nandi replied thoughtfully, "My people, they're dissatisfied, they're disillusioned, they're fed up, they're getting to the point of frustration where they are beginning to feel: What do we have to lose?"

Bonna interjected, "August told me that we are two societies, one black, one white."

My dad said, "Are we going to put *these two* through that?"

Nandi answered, "Its up to your people,"

My dad became irritated, saying, "Now wait a minute. I think this talk . . . tends to divide people, to build a wall in between people. All shortcomings are not the result of other people's aggressions."

Nandi proclaimed, "Race prejudice has shaped our history decisively; it now threatens to affect our future. The future of *these two*."

This was not good. My stomach got caught in a rip tide.

God, all I wanted was to be with Bonna. I thought Bonna was my gift… from You, God. Why are You punishing me for my feelings?

I began to well-up as they talked.

I burst, "Stop it! Leave us alone!"

I turned and I ran into the surf.

Bonna must have been as surprised as our parents must have been shocked.

Bonna paddled out to me.

Bonna sat up on her board and tried to joke, "Hey, freak show, are you ok?"

I replied, "God hates me. What did we do? God is prejudiced!" I sniveled.

Bonna quickly scolded me, "Don't you blaspheme!"

I declared, "Everyone is making this too hard. Screw everyone. *God* is making this too hard. We can plan for ourselves!"

Bonna warned me, "Now, don't you blaspheme!"

Bonna was really trying to calm me down. I realized that she cared.

I said, "I love you, Bonna."

Bonna hesitated then she said, "Of course you do!" and she grinned wickedly, quoting, "*Love, like rain, does not choose the grass on which it falls.*"

I asked, "Do you want me to go?"

Bonna replied softly, "No. I was talking about myself, too. But we are too young."

I said, "I won't tell anyone."

Bonna asked, "You're not going to write a Surrrf Dawgs song are you?"

I felt better.

Later, as my dad and I went home he puzzled at my silence.

Things got a little better after that but our parents kept their eyes on us.

One day on the phone I asked Bonna if she would like to come with me to look at the tide pools in Laguna Beach, south of Huntington Beach.

Bonna said, "Ex-cuse me?"

I explained that, "Tide pools are shallow pools of seawater that form on rocky shores. They are homes of cool sea creatures."

Bonna said, "Mmm hmmm."

I added, "We can go snorkeling too."

Bonna considered. Finally she said, "Ok. Snorkeling sounds ok."

So Bonna's mom brought her to Huntington as usual. Then my dad drove us farther south down to Laguna Beach. I gave Bonna my spare diving mask.

There at Laguna Beach my dad sat and studied his book as usual.

I explained to Bonna, "The water is only about 20 feet deep close to these rocks. But don't get hypnotized by all the cool stuff down there. The waves will take you right against the rocks. You can get really cut up!"

And so we swam along the rocky shore.

There was a wavy forest of kelp down below. There were some sea bass foraging. The current had shaped the sand bottom like ripples.

Bonna gave me an "Ok, cool" sign.

As we bobbed on around out of sight of any people we spotted a sandy grotto on shore.

Bonna said, " Let's check it out. Maybe it's a pirate cave!" and with a pirate accent she growled, "Yarrh, matey!" as she swam toward the big grotto.

The grotto was a long cave in the rocks with a silky sandy floor.

We pushed our masks back on our heads.

Walking past the opening it quickly became dark inside.

I said, "We don't want to get caught in here when the tide comes in."

Bonna took my hand and pressed warmly against me. I started to say something but she pressed her lips to my lips. With her tongue she opened my mouth.

I just held my mouth open as she rolled her tongue and she sought my tongue.

I finally understood the invitation.

Bonna ground her hips against my crotch. She pulled her mask off and then my mask.

We knelt down to the silky sand. She pushed me down and untied my swimming trunks. I pulled her bikini down. She straddled me and pushed my swollen penis into herself.

My fuse was lit and too short. I gasped in disbelief a couple of times and then I became disjointed, moaning in soul sucking acceleration.

Bonna stood up over me and wiggled, pulling her bikini bottom back up. She looked down at me and said, "The tide is coming in."

We located our masks.

We splashed out of the grotto and dove back into the surf.

When we returned to the beach at last, my father asked us, "Did you two have fun? See anything?"

I said, "We saw a lot."

My dad studied us.

Next day in my room with John I blurted, "We did it."

John asked casually, strumming his guitar, "Did what?"

I said, "It."

John repeated, "It?"

I confirmed with a nod and a grin, "It."

John asked, "Naw, dude. It?"

I said, "It as it gets"

John whooped, "You are officially a Dawg!" and he double picked some nonsense riff, howling like a dog.

I joined his yowling.

My mom called, "What kind of a song is that?!"

John and I yelled back, "The best!"

Then John said to me, "Details, details. Seriously."

I said, "I can't."

John said emphatically, "Try. Real. Hard."

I said, "Its too special."

John jumped up and wrestled me to the ground, pinning me. He puffed his cheeks and made sluicing loogie sounds above my face.

"Tell me," he threatened.

"Alright! Stop!" I pleaded.

And so I told John all the sacred details.

When I was finished, John slumped and whispered, "Whoa."

My balls ached.

Bonna started to call me more often but she still wouldn't give me her phone number.

Then one day she called me and she sounded worried.

I asked her, " Everything ok?"

She whispered, "I think I'm pregnant."

Silent thunder.

I became stupid, asking, "What? How?"

Bonna asked, upset, "How?!"

I asked, "What will we do?"

Bonna asked, "We?!"

I said, "Of course, we. We," and not knowing what possibly to say, I said, "God help us."

Bonna said, "I have to go," and she hung up as I was exclaiming, "Don't!"

I didn't hear from Bonna for weeks.

One day my mom answered the phone in the living room. I watched her from the kitchen. She said, "Yes. Oh, yes. Hello. Ok. What? What?! No. Oh, no. Oh, my God. Oh, my God," then she fell into the chair, holding her head.

My mom hollered for my dad, "Don. Come here!"

My dad answered, "What is it?"

My mom said urgently, "Come here *now.*"

My parents spoke softly together in hurried words. My dad then turned toward me and glared. My mom started to cry.

My dad took the phone and was growling, trying to sound restrained. My mom looked at me and whispered, "Do you know what you've done? What were you thinking, Dean?"

My dad finally hung up the phone, turned to me, and commanded, "Come here this second!"

Standing over me my dad cursed me, asking me, "Do you realize what a goddamn fuck up you are?!"

My mom admonished my dad, "Don…"

My dad continued, and I thought he was going to hit me. He said, "Do you have any sense? Look what you have done to your mother,…to me,…to yourself!"

I cowered and I whimpered, "I'm sorry, I'm sorry…"

I moved toward my mom but she raised her hand, saying, "Don't touch me!"

My dad hollered, "I hope you know that you have ruined Bonna's life! You idiot! How can you be *our* son?! "

I cried, "I have not ruined Bonna's life! God will help us."

My dad grabbed my arm and he yelled in my face, "You just leave God out of your sin! You just pray that you can be forgiven!"

Then my dad said, "You and Bonna are *done*! We're going to handle this with her parents and you're going to pray they don't sue us!"

For the next week my mom and dad ground me into embers.

John tip-toed over to visit me. He said, "Dude, even Jesus was only in Hell for three days."

I moaned, "That doesn't help me, John. I'm a father. A father, dude. I looked up pictures of babies in jars."

John asked, "What are they gonna do?"

I revealed, "I heard my dad talking about ending… ending the pregnancy."

John mused, then he was asking, "Does anyone, like, even care what you say?"

I replied, "My mom asked Pastor Laurence to come to our house."

John was hopeful, saying, "Pastor Laurence was pretty cool to me once when I, like, pretended to snore during his sermon."

Nobody cared about what I felt when Pastor Laurence did come over. He asked me to go to my room and pray. But I eavesdropped while he was counseling my mom and dad.

Pastor Laurence was saying, "As American Baptists we oppose abortion as a means of avoiding responsibility for conception. We oppose abortion as a primary means of birth control. And we oppose abortion without regard for the far-reaching consequences of the act."

Pastor Laurence emphasized, "We also denounce irresponsible sexual behavior."

So I was denounced by our church. I completely lost hope. I was damned to Hell and so was Bonna. And so was our kid. Why, God? You made me love Bonna. Now You make us evil?

Pastor Laurence concluded, "Recognizing that each person is ultimately responsible to God, we do encourage men and women in these circumstances to seek spiritual counsel as they prayerfully and conscientiously consider their decision."

My parents thanked Pastor Laurence and he departed.

My mom and dad barely spoke to me. I knew that if not for my mom then my dad would have beaten me the way he said that his dad used to beat him.

A week later the phone rang. My mom answered. She said loudly, "No, you cannot speak to him. You are not supposed to call here *at all*. What?" and then my mom stopped talking and she listened intently for several minutes.

Then my mom called me to the phone and said, "Bonna has something for you to hear."

My mom stood over me.

I eagerly took the phone, asking, "Bonna, are you alright?"

I looked up at my mom as I dared to say, "I miss you, I am so sorry."

Bonna answered with restrained emotion, "I'm keeping the baby. But I have to go live with my grandma and grandpa in Detroit."

I asked, "When can we see each other again?" and I stared defiantly at my mom who said nothing.

Bonna answered, "I agreed I would give our…the baby for adoption. That is for the best," and Bonna started to sob.

I started to cry.

Bonna then said, "We can't see each other for a long time. I have to go."

The clack of her receiver was a like a gunshot.

My mom took the phone from me and hung up the phone for me.

Then my mom hugged me silently.

And so a long grim year came and crawled slowly over me.

At last, one day when I was home alone, the phone rang. I picked it up.

I cried, "Bonna! Where are you?"

She didn't sound the same as she told me, "I'm still in Detroit. Dean…," and her tone of voice made my heart sink but I didn't know why.

Bonna said, "Dean, I met someone who says he wants to marry me, to take care of my boy,… our boy. He has a good job at the Ford plant. I can keep my boy…"

I broke down, "What? What?"

Bonna replied, "Oh, Dean, I named him Shaka Dean Natali."

I repeated, "Shaka Dean Natali? You're going to marry…?"

Donna said, "Dean,… it's the only way to keep Shaka Dean…keep my son. The only way."

I exclaimed, "But I lose everything!"

"The only way," Bonna cried and she broke my heart forever when she disconnected.

I lost my adolescence.

Now I always think of Bonna but I haven't heard from her again.

My parents and me never speak of Bonna. Sometimes we just look at each other.

During the L.A. riots I thought about Bonna's brother, August.

Oh, and John got expelled for marijuana. My parents said that I could not see him anymore but I did.

We smoke a lot of marijuana together.

And I am born again. I baptize myself surfing all the time. I stopped praying, I stopped giving thanks. God does what He wants.

#

Rerences:

1) https://www.nydailynews.com/news/national/birmingham-erupted-chaos-1963-battle-civil-rights-exploded-south-article-1.1071793
2) https://www.newyorker.com/culture/the-front-row/what-to-stream-james-baldwins-tour-of-black-san-francisco-in-take-this-hammer

3) https://www.newyorker.com/magazine/2020/06/22/the-history-
    of-the-riot-report?fbclid=IwAR2quA3mh-
    lx2G2AHpNNok8i_5kwUrdC9ylmm5HinXnzkXfRuHwrmHZ
    kLbk

4) https://en.wikipedia.org/wiki/Tide_pool

5) https://www.pewforum.org/2013/01/16/religious-groups-
    official-positions-on-abortion/

6) https://www.wikihow.com/Surf